ES LA HORA OTRA VEZ.

¿Estás listo?

TOCA LA MANCHA GRIS. MUY LEVEMENTE,
PARA VER LO QUE PASA.

¡AHÍ ESTÁN!

PERO, ¿NO TE PARECEN UN POCO TÍMIDAS?
TÓCALA OTRA VEZ. TOCA, TOCA, TOCA.

¡Aquí vienen!

PERO TODAVÍA FALTAN ALGUNAS.
PRUEBA A TOCARLA SOLAMENTE UNA VEZ MÁS.

¡AL FIN! TODAS ESTÁN AQUÍ. ASÍ QUE AHORA . . .

PON TU MANO SOBRE LA PÁGINA, CIERRA LOS OJOS
Y CUENTA HASTA CINCO.

¡SÍ! ¡TÚ TIENES EL TOQUE MÁGICO!

¡VAMOS A MEZCLARLO BIEN!

CON UN DEDO, TOMA UN POQUITO DEL AZUL . . .

Y TOCA EL AMARILLO UN POQUITO. FROTA . . . SUAVECITO . . .

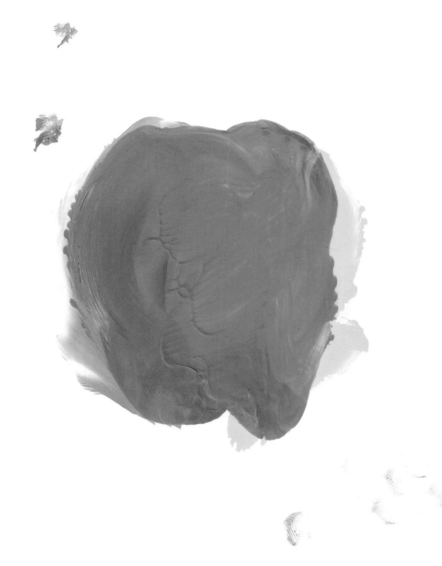

¿LO VES?

AHORA, TOMA UN POQUITÍN DEL ROJO . . .

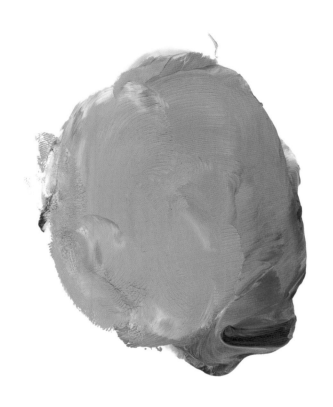

Y FRÓTALO SOBRE EL AZUL.

¿DE ACUERDO?

PRUEBA A TOMAR UN POCO DE ESE AMARiLLO . . .

Y UNTARLO ENCIMA DEL ROJO.

¡Estupendo! ¿Puedes recordar todo eso?

Entonces, vamos a divertirnos.

¿Quieres seguir? ¡De acuerdo!

Agita el libro bien fuerte.

¿Qué crees que va a pasar?

¡Exacto!

AHORA PRUEBA A INCLINAR EL LIBRO HACIA LA DERECHA.

¿Qué crees que va a pasar?

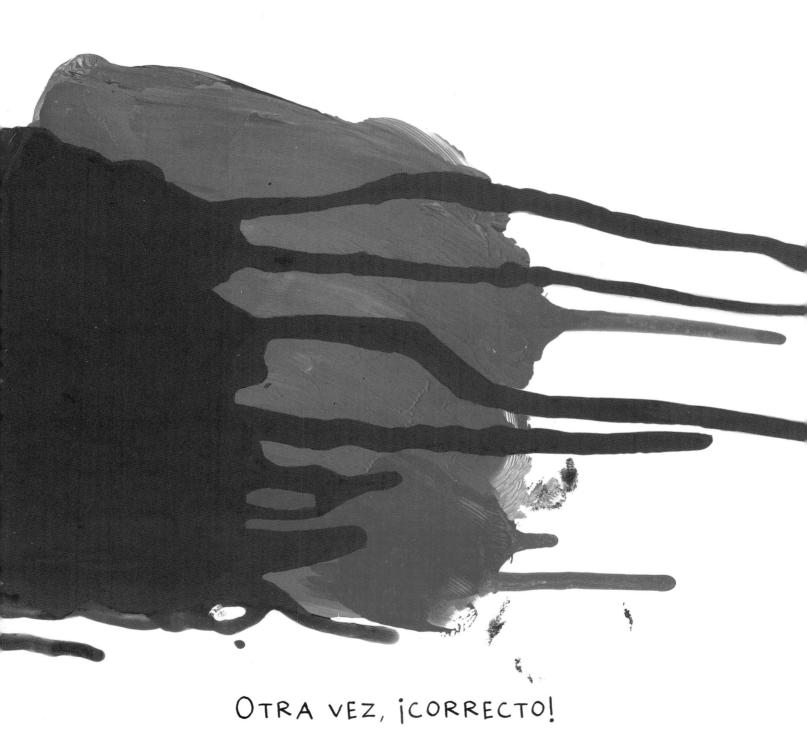

Otra vez, ¡correcto!

CiERRA EL LiBRO Y PRESiÓNALO BiEN FUERTE . . .

PARA QUE LOS COLORES SE MEZCLEN BIEN . . .

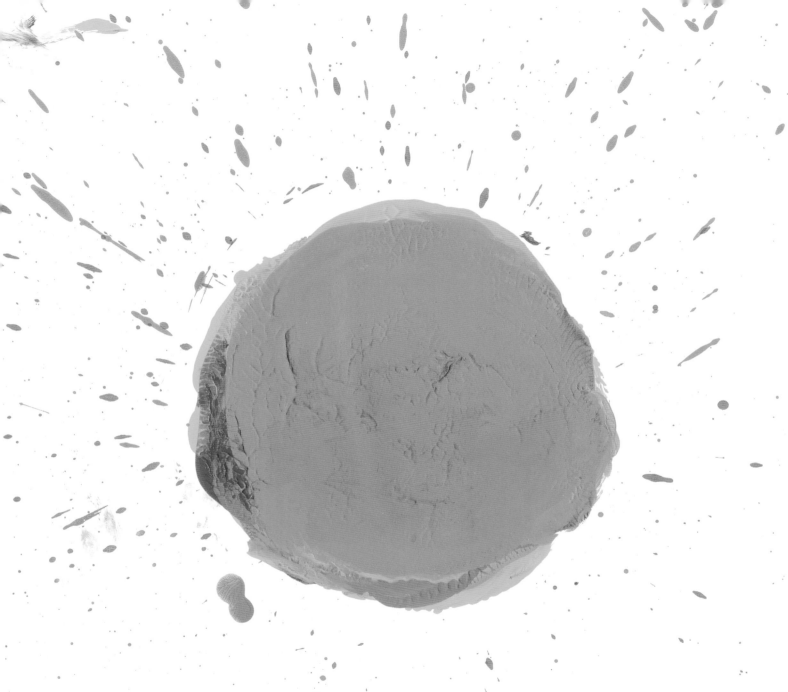

¿ESO PENSABAS?

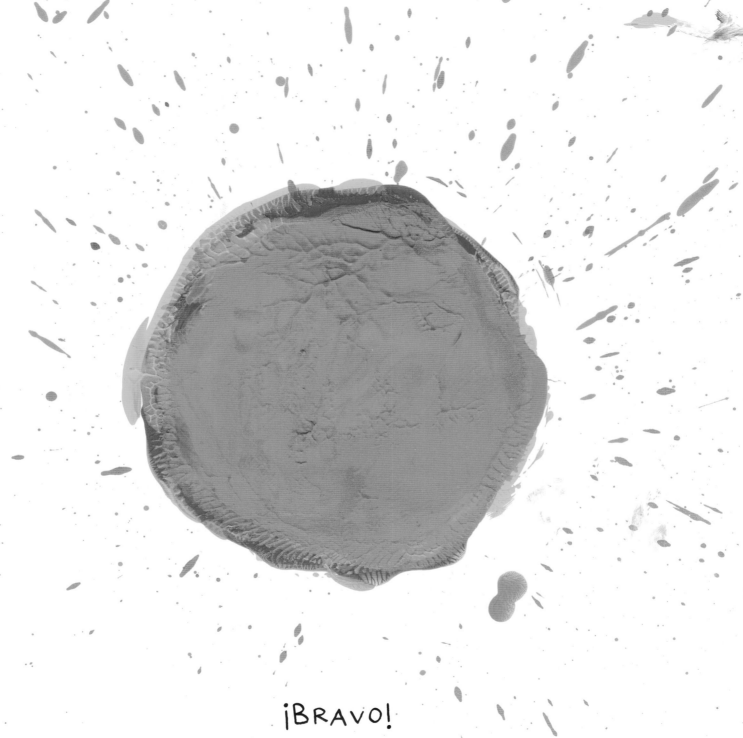

¡BRAVO!

Si FROTAS LOS DOS COLORES UNO CON EL OTRO BiEN FUERTE...

ENTONCES, ¿QUÉ PASA?

¡Eso mismo!

Y PARA QUE TODAS ESAS MANCHAS SE VUELVAN VERDES,

¿QUÉ ES LO QUE TIENES QUE HACER?

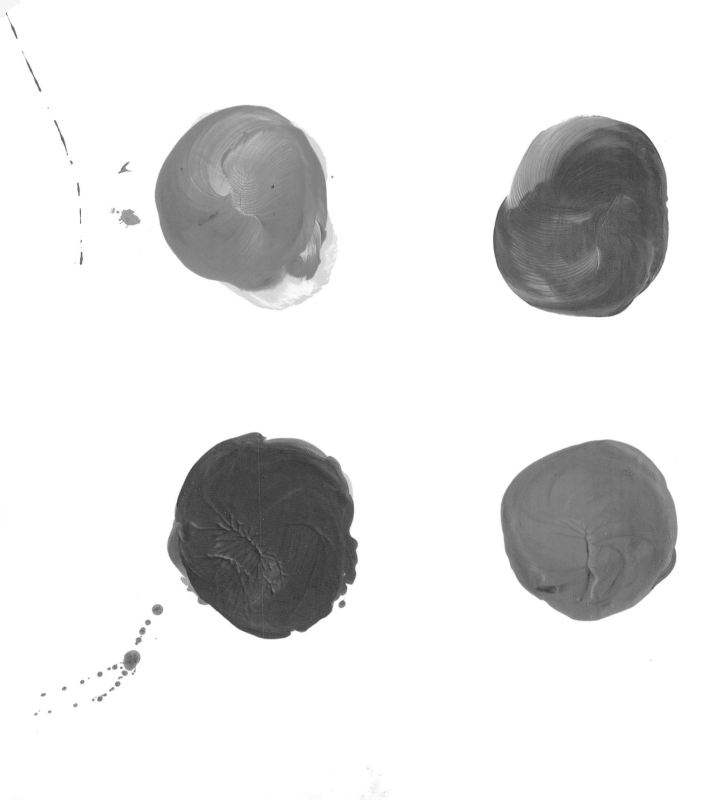

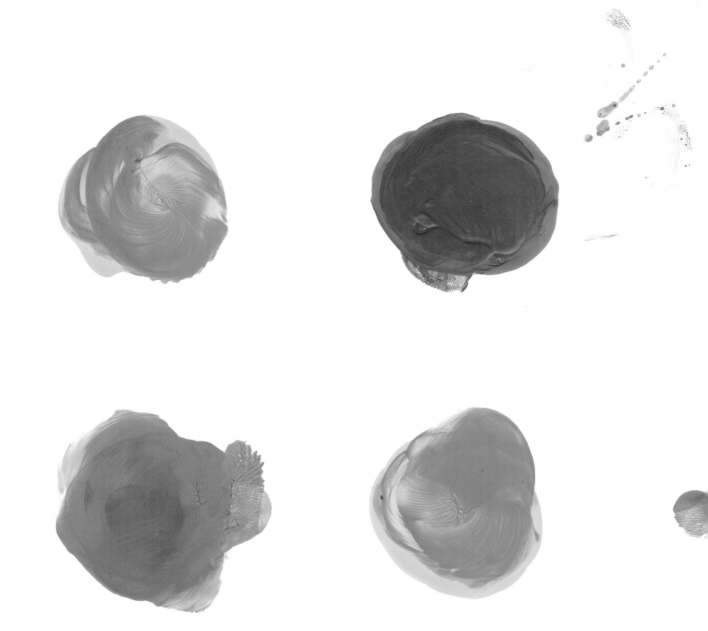

¡Sí! ¡Muy bien!

¿MÁS?

EL BLANCO HACE LOS COLORES MÁS PÁLIDOS.

DALE, ¡PRUÉBALO!

¿LO VES?

Y EL NEGRO LOS HACE MÁS OSCUROS.

¡PRUEBA OTRA VEZ!

¿ENTENDISTE? TIENE SENTIDO, ¿NO ES VERDAD?

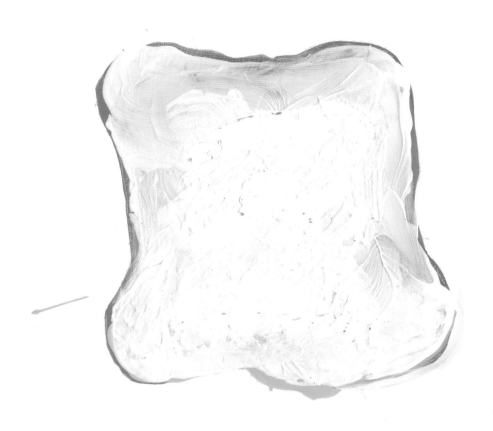

ASÍ QUE SI TÚ APRETUJAS ESTAS DOS PÁGINAS JUNTAS . . .

(¡NO TIENES MÁS QUE CERRAR RÁPIDO EL LIBRO!)

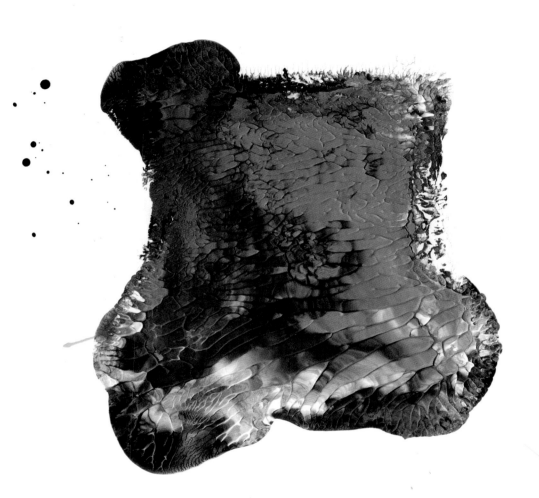

. . . ¡ESTO ES LO QUE VA A PASAR!

ESO ES TODO. LO ENTENDISTE. ¡TODO LISTO!

SÓLO UNA COSA MÁS:

PON LA MANO SOBRE LA PÁGINA, Y . . .

CUENTA HASTA CINCO . . .

¡Hasta luego!

AHORA, ¡A JUGAR POR TU CUENTA!

MIRA,

JUEGA, Y

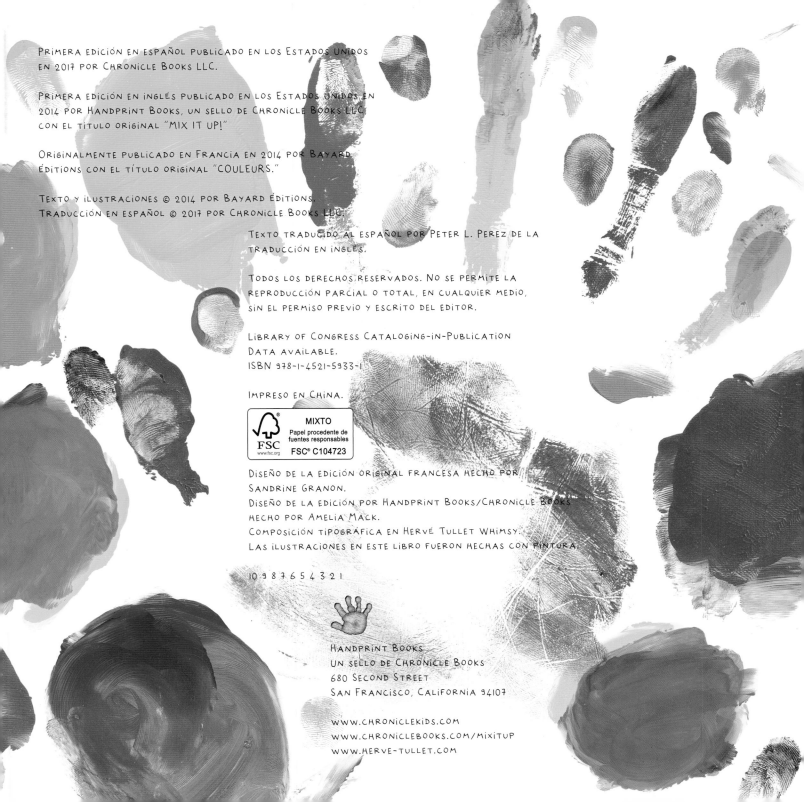

Primera edición en español publicado en los Estados Unidos en 2017 por Chronicle Books LLC.

Primera edición en inglés publicado en los Estados Unidos en 2014 por Handprint Books, un sello de Chronicle Books LLC con el título original "MIX IT UP!"

Originalmente publicado en Francia en 2014 por Bayard Éditions con el título original "COULEURS."

Library of Congress Cataloging-in-Publication Data available.
ISBN 978-1-4521-5933-1

Impreso en China.

MIXTO
Papel procedente de fuentes responsables
FSC
www.fsc.org
FSC® C104723

Diseño de la edición original francesa hecho por Sandrine Granon.
Diseño de la edición por Handprint Books/Chronicle Books hecho por Amelia Mack.
Composición tipográfica en Hervé Tullet Whimsy.
Las ilustraciones en este libro fueron hechas con pintura.

10 9 8 7 6 5 4 3 2 1

Handprint Books
Un sello de Chronicle Books
680 Second Street
San Francisco, California 94107

www.chroniclekids.com
www.chroniclebooks.com/mixitup
www.herve-tullet.com

GRIMERICKS

by Susan Pearson

illustrated by Gris Grimly

Marshall Cavendish Children

To Tony D.

Life is like a burned pot of macaroni and cheese.

It all tastes good until you get to the bottom.

—G.G.

For Alice

—S.P.

Marshall Cavendish Corporation
99 White Plains Road, Tarrytown, NY 10591
www.marshallcavendish.us

Text copyright © 2005 by Susan Pearson
Illustrations copyright © 2005 by Gris Grimly

Library of Congress Cataloging-in-Publication Data

Pearson, Susan.
Grimericks / by Susan Pearson ; illustrated by Gris Grimly.
p. cm.
ISBN 0-7614-5230-3
1. Limericks, Juvenile. 2. Children's poetry, American.
I. Grimly, Gris. II. Title.
PS3566.E23435G75 2005
811'.54—dc22
2004025518

The text of this book is set in Regula.
The illustrations are rendered in watercolor and ink.
Book design by Adam Mietlowski

Printed in China

First edition
3 5 6 4 2

Dear Reader, please lend me your ear.
If ghosts, ghouls, and goblins you fear,
   don't open this book.
   No—don't even look!
There are spooky things hiding in here.

Millicent Mooney is dead.
At least that's what everyone said.
She's had nothing to say
for a month and a day,
and a stork's built a nest on her head.

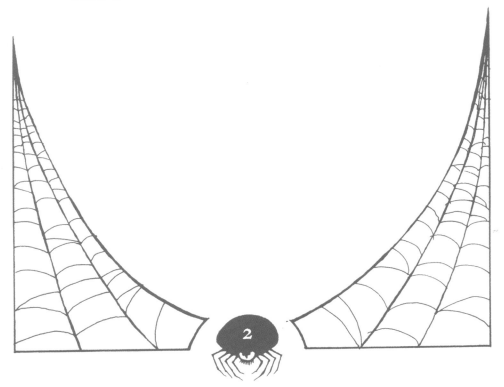

2

The goblins are gobblin' tonighten—
a-gnashin', a-gnawin', a-bitin',
a-spittin', a-slurpin',
a-belchin', a-burpin'—
their manners are very a-frightnin'!

A goblin in T-shirt and jeans
was fond of a diner in Queens.
He ordered spook-etti,
fang-furters, roast yeti,
and then, for dessert, human beans.

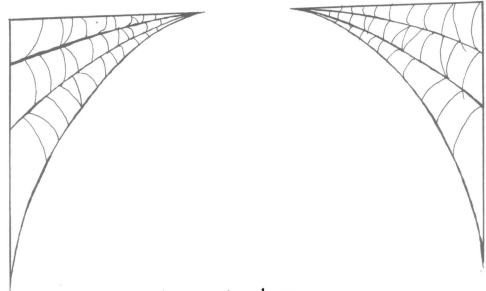

Boris the boy-eating bear
is haunting the seventeenth stair.
He likes to devour
a boy every hour.
If you hear something growling, beware!

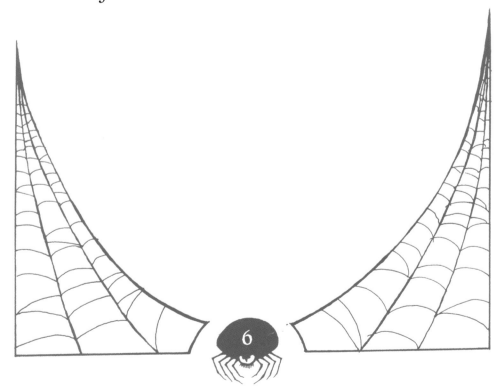

A witch named Bettina von Spike
had neither a broom nor a bike . . .
    nor a car, nor a truck—
    she was quite out of luck.
Poor Bettina was forced to witchhike.

Priscilla the witch is a scandal.

Her spells can't light even a candle.

Her wand is all rusted.

Her broom is half busted.

No wonder she flies off the handle.

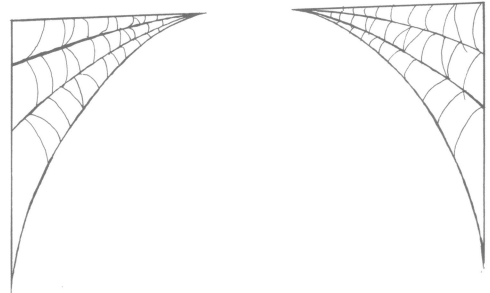

A ghost in our bathroom, Glen Gower,
brushes his teeth on the hour,
turns the cold water hot,
drops my socks in the pot,
and sings while I'm taking a shower.

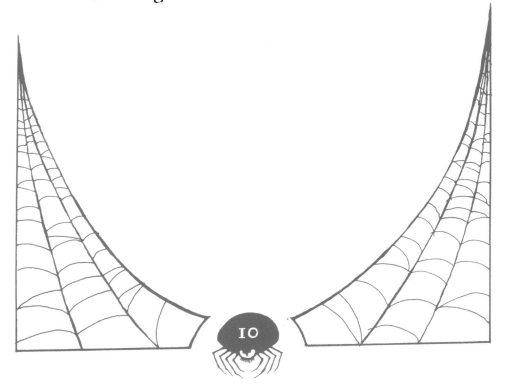

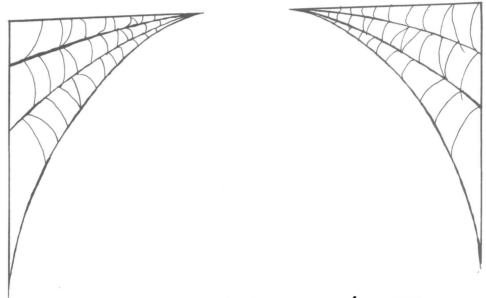

Beware that you don't get too chummy
with Martin McIver the mummy.
He has termites and moths
inside of his cloths,
and he'd rather have YOU in his tummy.

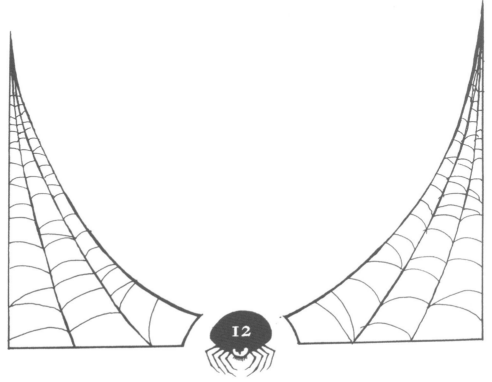

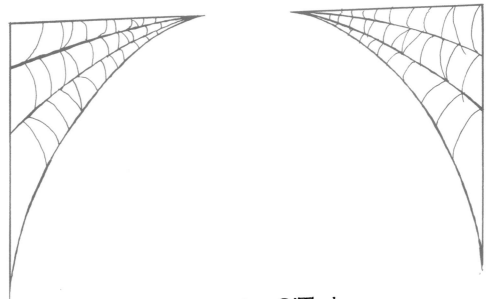

A banshee named Mrs. O'Toole
teaches wailing at Spookytime School,
Mr. Bones teaches dances,
Ms. Ghost teaches trances,
and grades are passed out by Miss Ghoul.

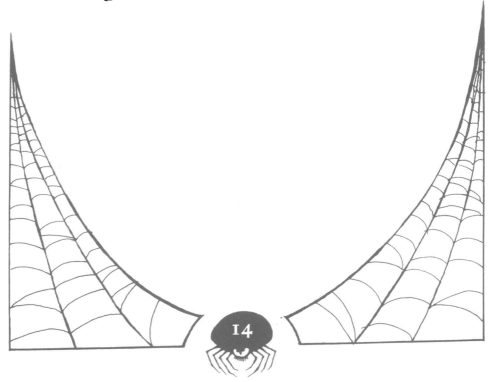

A skeleton, MaryLou Jones,
only yawns and grumbles and groans
when she's asked in Seattle
to shake, rock, and rattle.
They've nicknamed her Lazybones Jones.

When Howard the goblin caught sight
of Gertrude the gremlin one night,
    he fell in a swoon
    that lasted till June.
It must have been love at first fright.

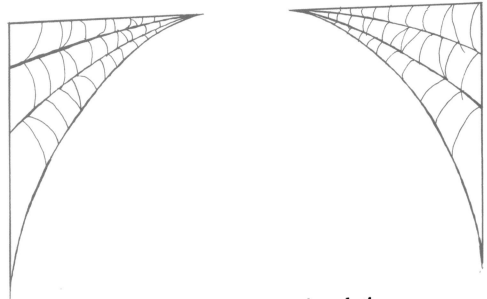

Augustus, a ghoul who played chess,
felt his game was a howling success.
If a player could beat him,
then Gus would just eat him.
"Too bad," he said. "One player less."

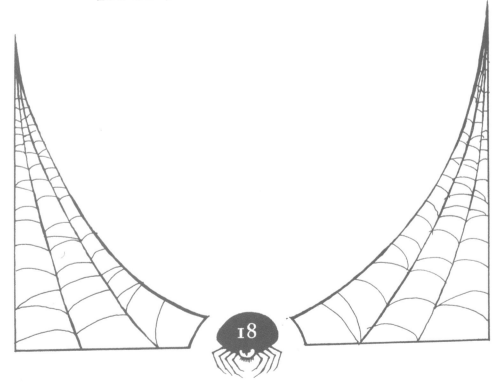

18

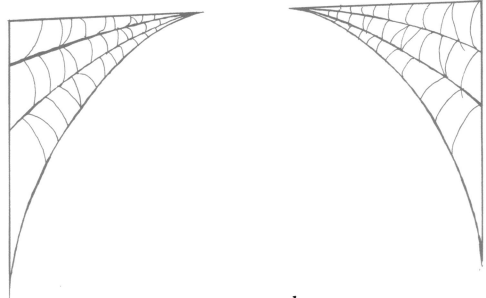

Whenever you open our door,
you are likely to hear a loud snore.
It's a ghost named King Kong,
but his name is all wrong!
He just sleeps all day long—what a bore!

20

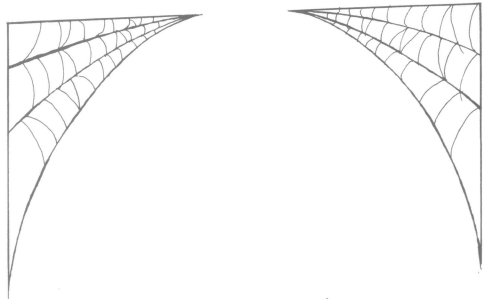

Two witches who live past the gates
have scooters and bikes and some skates
but one broom between them.
Perhaps you have seen them
in flight. They are perfect broom-mates.

22

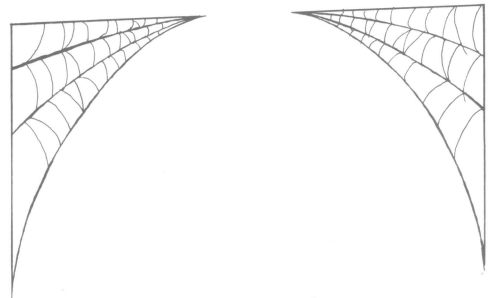

The lawn is crawling with cats.
In the cellar are fifty-three rats.
The curtains are lace,
but the tub's a disgrace
and the toilet is brimming with bats!

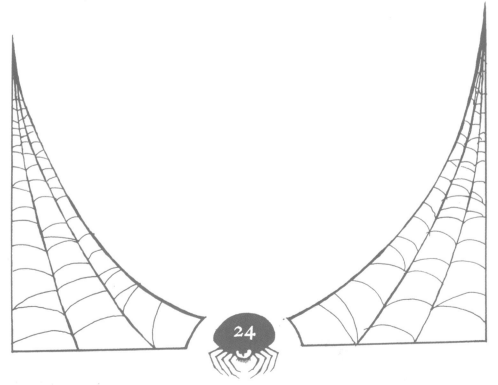

There are skeleton horses out west
who deliver the mail without rest.
They ride night and day.
I heard someone say
his letter was bony expressed.

26

When Gary the ghost goes to school,
all you can see is his drool.
    It drips off the clock,
        down the walls, from the chalk.
I think that there should be a rule!

Wanda the witchling was wary
of anything fuzzy or hairy.
Beavers and bats,
gorillas and cats,
and cows were especially scary.

If Grace sees a ball, she will throw it.
A trumpet? A sax? She will blow it!
    She cannot be seen,
    but she thinks she's the queen,
and she wants to make sure that you know it.